AUG 2 9 2013
P9-DMO-791
NAPA CITY-COUNTY LIBRARY
580 COOMBS STREET
NAPA, CA 94559

To Wilfrid Wood

Copyright © 2012 by David Lucas

All rights reserved. No part of this book may be reproduced, transmitted, or stored in an information retrieval system in any form or by any means, graphic, electronic, or mechanical, including photocopying, taping, and recording, without prior written permission from the publisher.

First U.S. edition 2013

Library of Congress Catalog Card Number 2012942674

ISBN 978-0-7636-6107-6

13 14 15 16 17 18 CCP 10 9 8 7 6 5 4 3 2

Printed in Shenzhen, Guangdong, China

This book was typeset in Berkeley Old Style.
The illustrations were done in ink and watercolor.

Candlewick Press
99 Dover Street
Somerville, Massachusetts 02144

visit us at www.candlewick.com

Candlewick Press

THE SKELETON PIRATE
David
Lucas

Everyone had heard of the Skeleton Pirate.
The Skeleton Pirate was the Terror of the Seas.

"I'll never be beaten!" he said.

“I’ll never be beaten!”

“I’ll NEVER be beaten!”

All the other pirates cheered.
"We've beaten the Skeleton Pirate at last!"
"*Curses!*" said the Skeleton Pirate through gritted teeth.
"I'll never be beaten!"

"Hahaha!" they laughed, and threw him overboard.

"Hello there, my lovely!" said the Skeleton Pirate.
The Mermaid smiled. "Oh dear! It looks like you've been beaten at last!"
"I'll never be beaten!" he said. "Would you . . . ? Oh, thank you, my dear . . ."

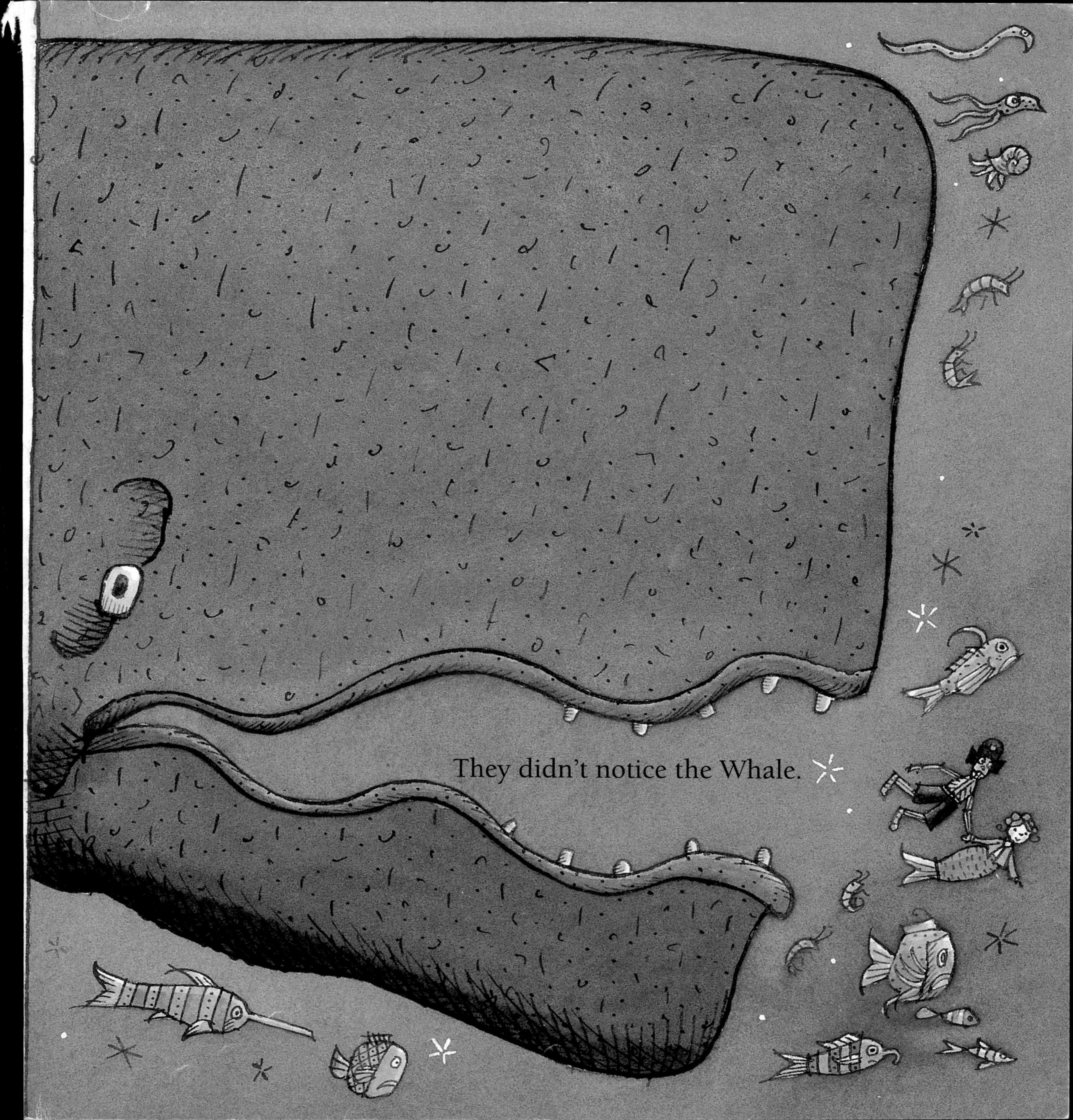

They didn’t notice the Whale.

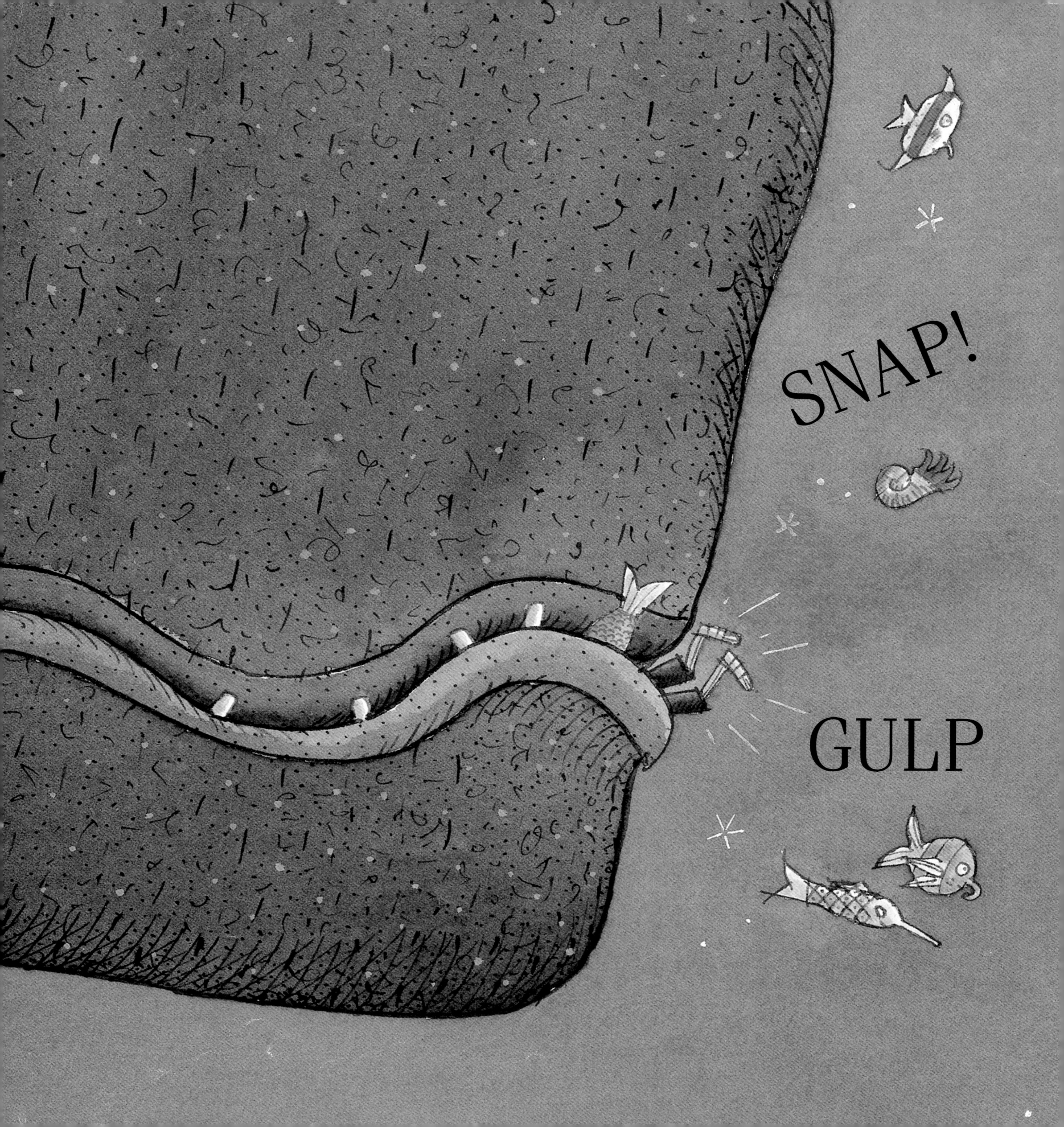
SNAP!
GULP

"What do we do now?" cried the Mermaid.
They were in the belly of the Whale.
"We're not beaten yet!" said the Skeleton Pirate,
and he shook his fist.
"Hey, Whale! Come and fight me, you big coward!"

But the only sound was the Mermaid
blowing her nose.

"Perhaps fighting isn't always the answer," said the Mermaid gently.

"What else is there?" said the Skeleton Pirate.

"*Talking?*" said the Mermaid.

"Talking!" said the Skeleton Pirate. "Of course!"

They looked at each other.

"But I don't think the Whale can hear us," said the Skeleton Pirate.

"We could speak right in his ear," said the Mermaid.

"Where's the ear of a whale?"

"Right near his brain," said the Mermaid.

"Come on!" The Skeleton Pirate flashed his eyes. "I've got a plan!"

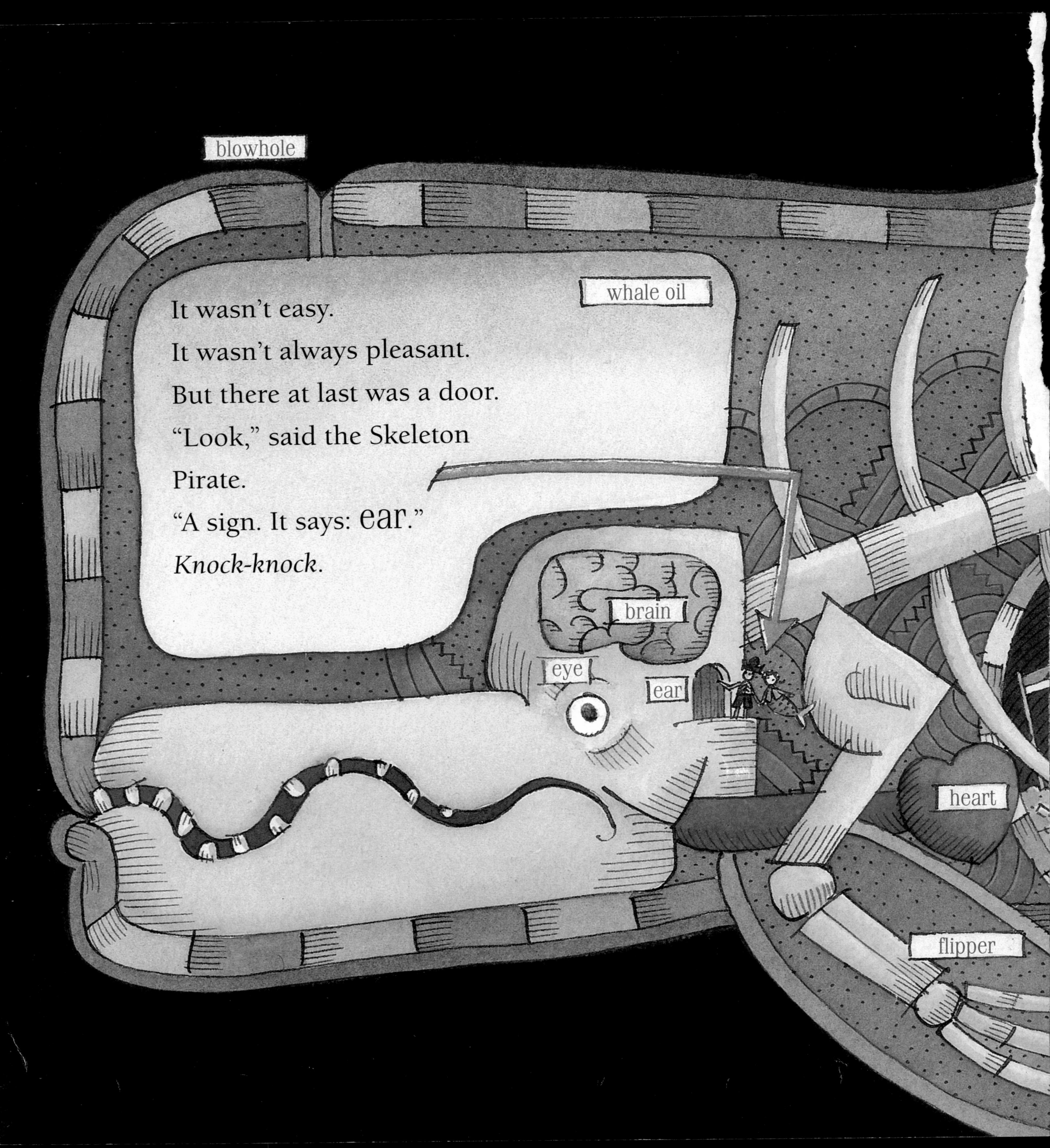

It wasn't easy.

It wasn't always pleasant.

But there at last was a door.

"Look," said the Skeleton Pirate.

"A sign. It says: ear."

Knock-knock.

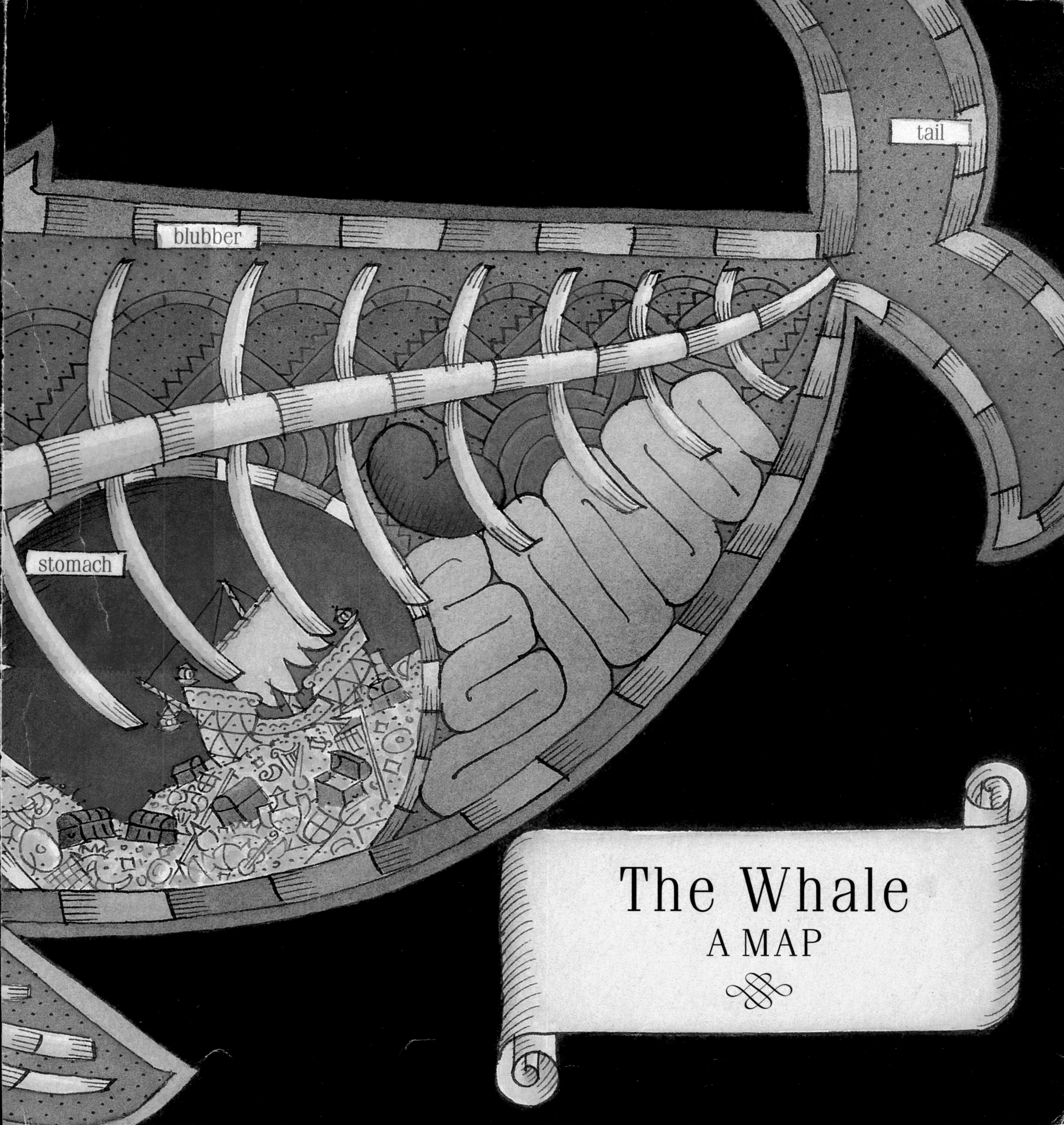
tail
blubber
stomach
The Whale
A MAP

"Who's there?" boomed the Whale.

"You *ate* us," said the Skeleton Pirate.

"You swallowed us whole."

"Oh dear, I'm terribly sorry," said the Whale. His voice echoed all around them.

"Did you know you're full of gold and treasure and jewels?" said the Skeleton Pirate.

"You even swallowed a *Golden Ship*!" said the Mermaid.

"No wonder I feel so ill," said the Whale. "I wish there was *something* somebody could do to help."

The Skeleton Pirate grinned. "I know exactly what to do."

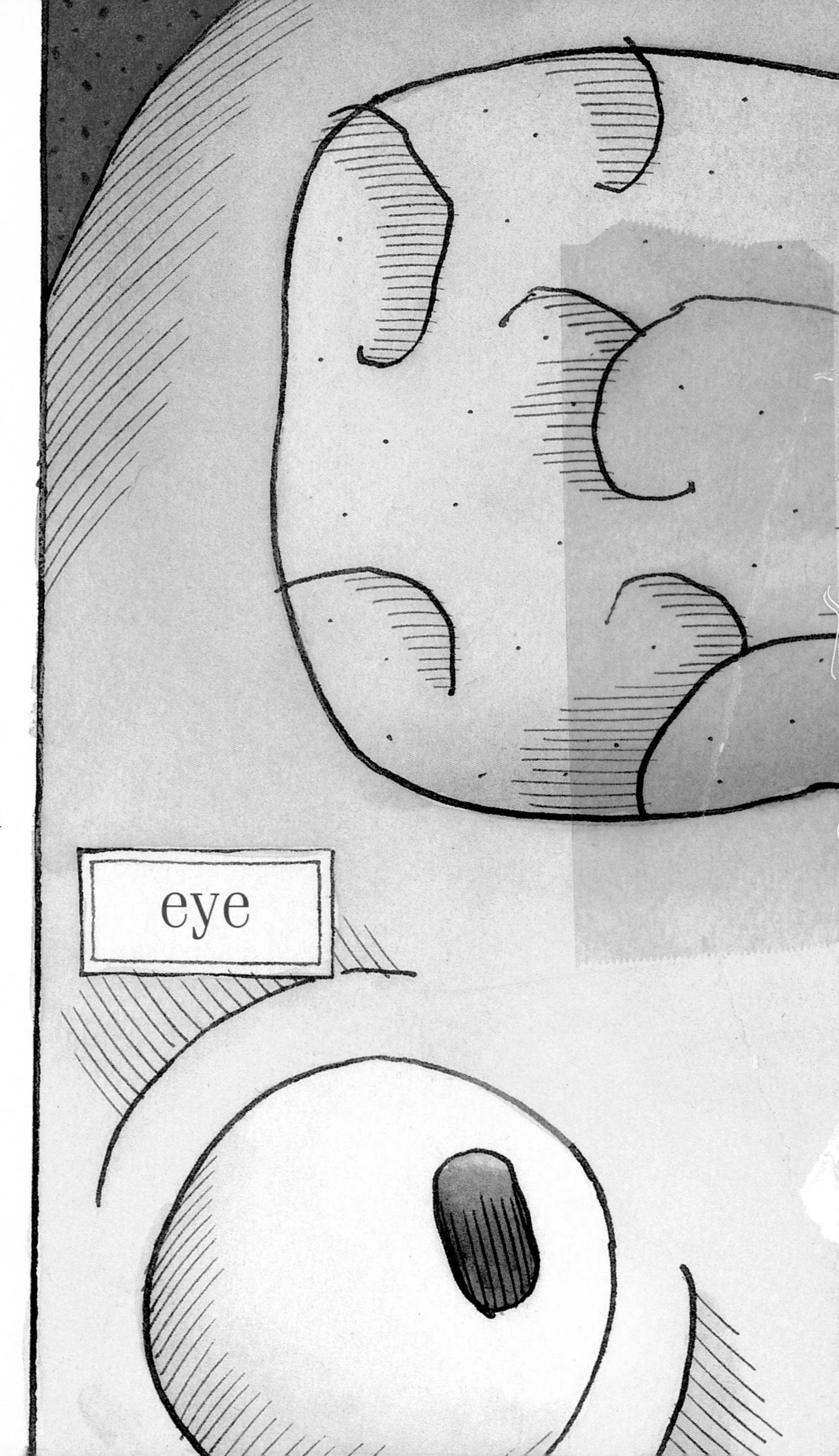

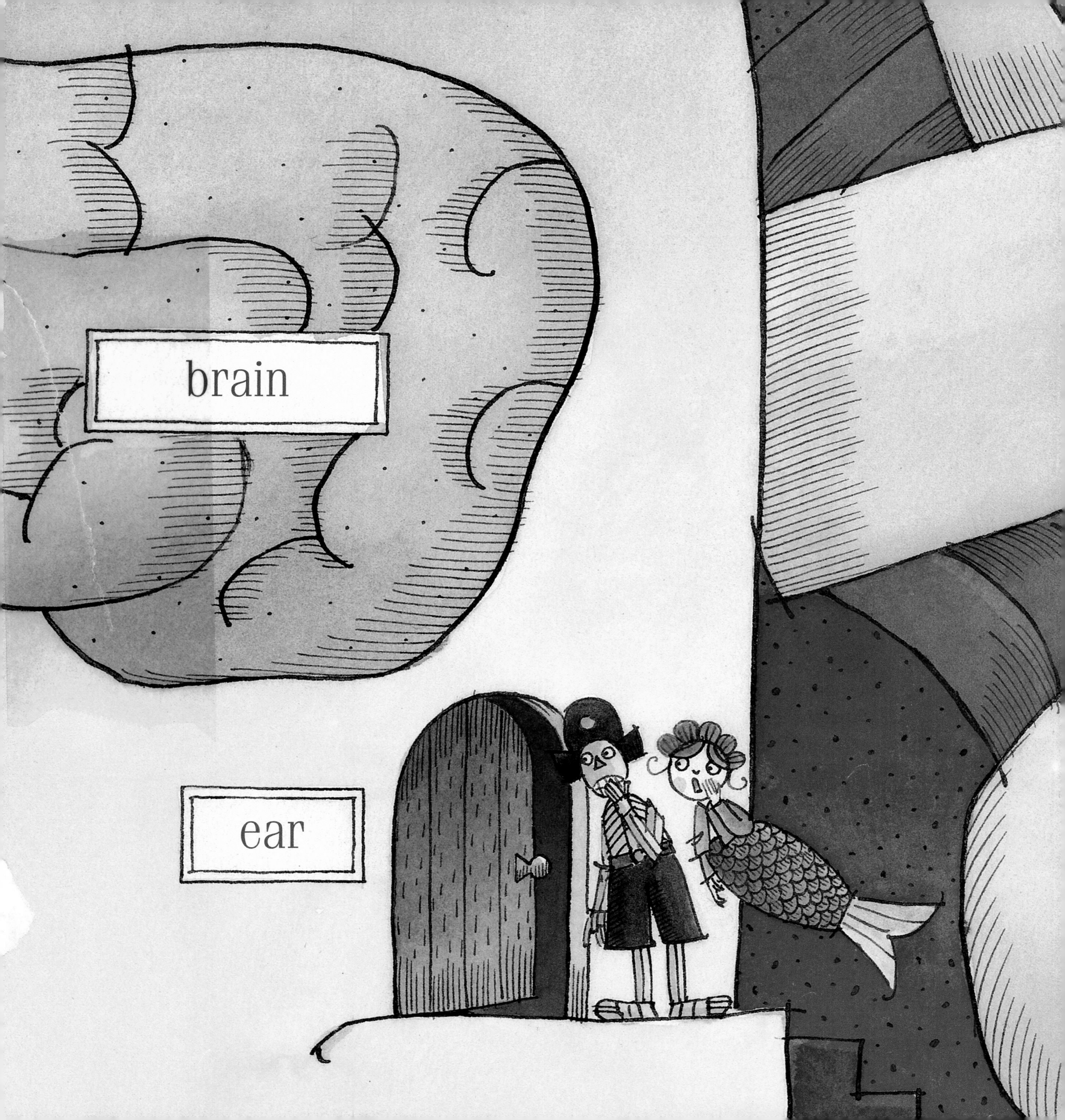
brain
ear

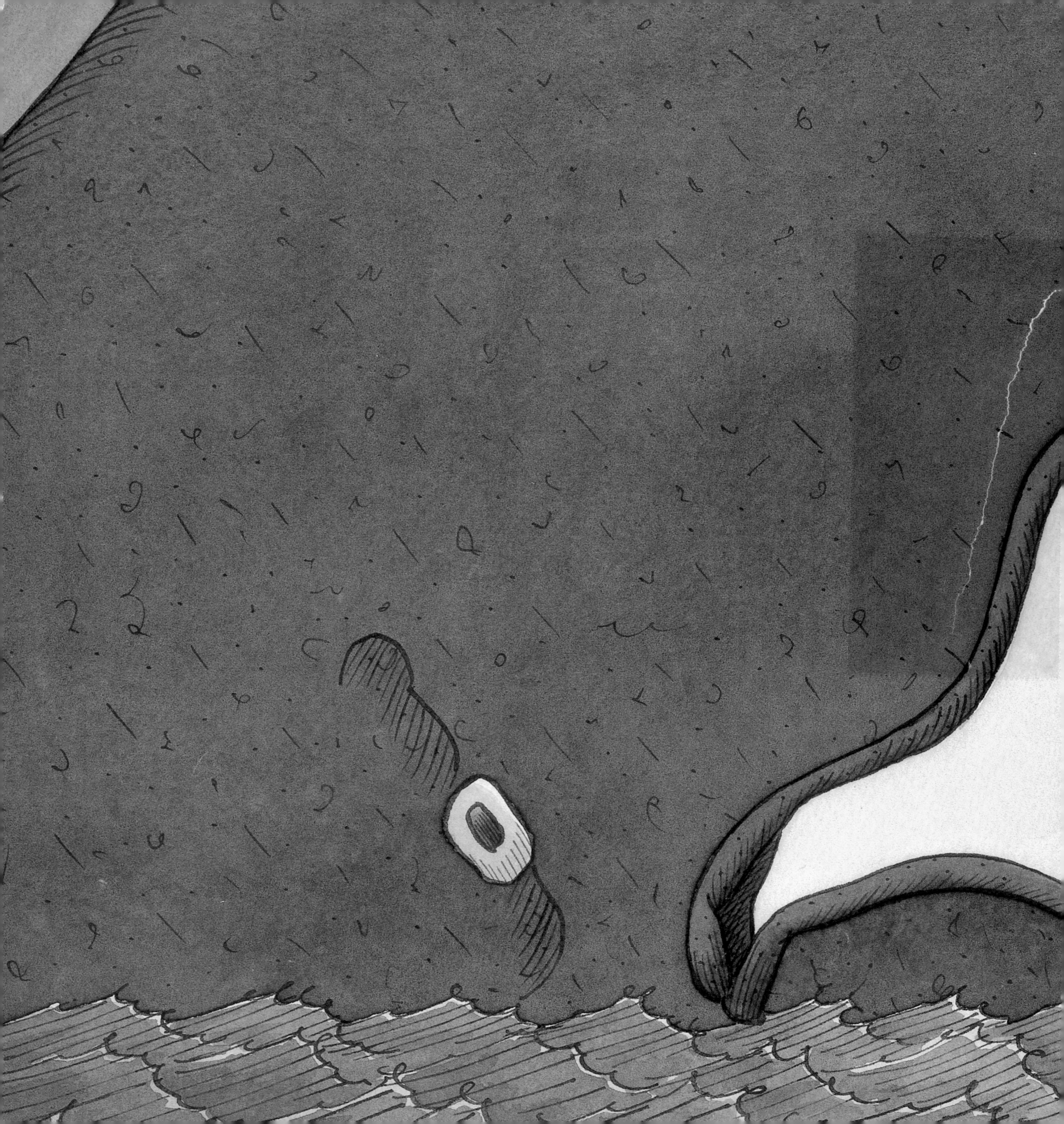

They filled the Golden Ship with treasure.
"Open wide!" cried the Skeleton Pirate.
The Whale did as he was told.

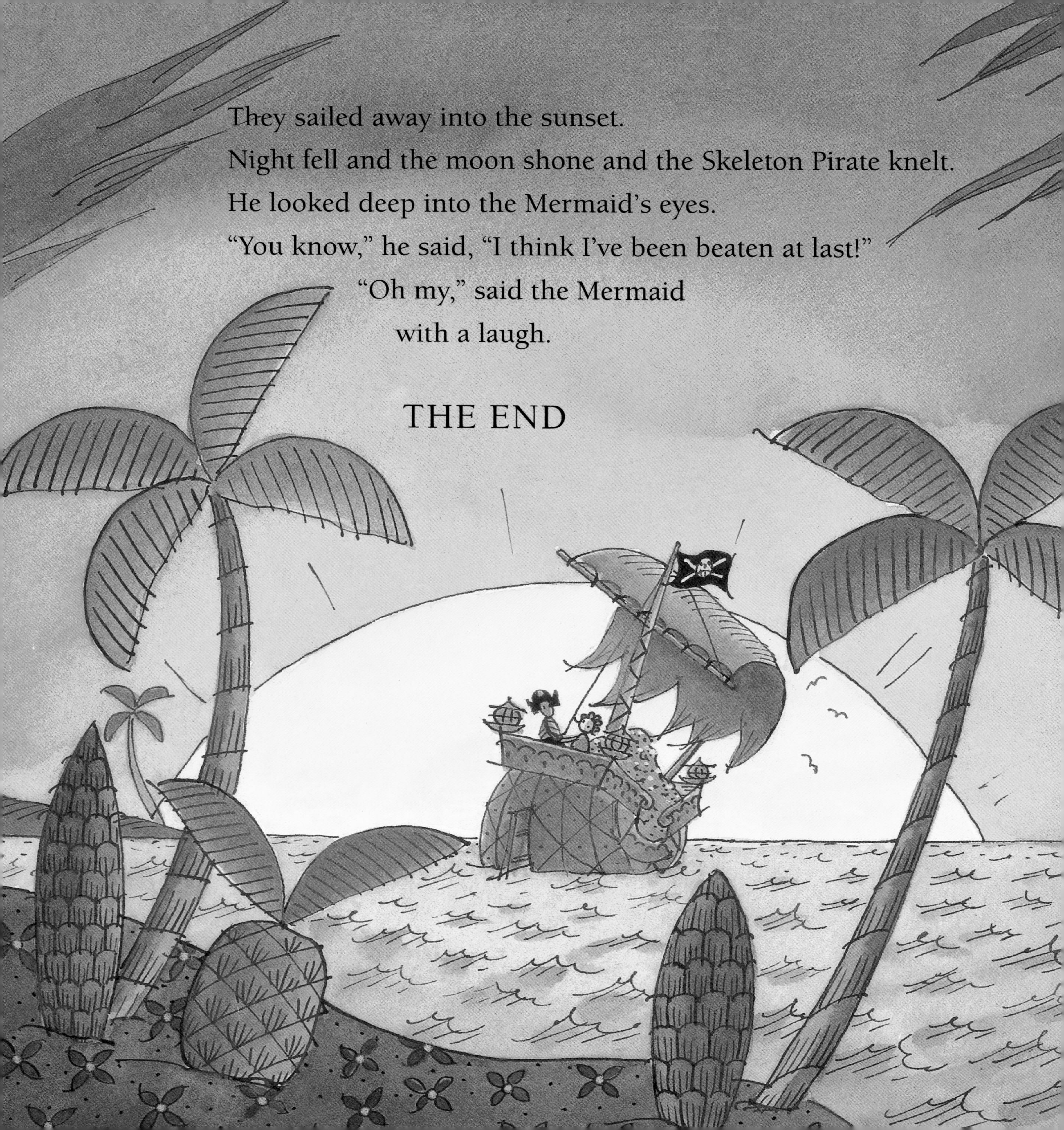

They sailed away into the sunset.
Night fell and the moon shone and the Skeleton Pirate knelt.
He looked deep into the Mermaid's eyes.
"You know," he said, "I think I've been beaten at last!"
"Oh my," said the Mermaid
with a laugh.

THE END